Dolly Takes a Drive

Elizabeth Kernan

NEIGHBORHOOD READERS

Rosen Classroom Books & Materials™

New York

Dolly and Kate went for a drive.

Dolly said, "I see a school."

Kate said, "I see a red light."

"Look! I see a cow by the barn,"
said Dolly.

"I see a picnic table," said Kate.
"We can eat here."

"I see bikes," said Dolly.

"Look! I see a playground,"
said Kate.
"We can play," said Dolly.

They went down the road again.

"Look! I see the swimming
pool sign," said Kate.

"We can go swimming!"
said Dolly.

Then Dolly and Kate went home.